Go, Dog. Go!

Paw-some Pals

By Mary Man-Kong

Illustrated by Alan Batson

A GOLDEN BOOK · NEW YORK

© 2021 DHX-Go Dog Go Productions Inc. Based on the book *Go, Dog. Go!*
by P.D. Eastman © P.A. Eastman Revocable Trust and Alan Eastman LLC.

Published in the United States by Random House Children's Books, a division of Penguin Random House LLC,
1745 Broadway, New York, NY 10019, and in Canada by Penguin Random House Canada Limited, Toronto.
Golden Books, A Golden Book, and the G colophon are registered trademarks of Penguin Random House LLC.

ISBN 978-0-593-37349-1 (trade)

rhcbooks.com

PENCIL MANUFACTURED IN TAIWAN

Book printed in the United States of America

10 9 8 7 6 5 4 3 2 1

This is Tag Barker.
She loves making things go!

Tag has a new neighbor.

To find out his name, follow the lines and
write each letter in the correct box.

O H C S C O

Tag is a good friend.
She always lends a helping paw.

**Scooch used to live on a farm.
He loves chickens.**

Starting at the arrow, go clockwise and write every other letter in the blanks to find out what Tag is saying.

⬜⬜, ⬜⬜⬜. ⬜⬜!

Use the key to find out the name of Tag and Scooch's town.

O	T	N	S	W	P	A

___ ___ ___ ___ ___ ___ ___

ANSWER: Pawston.

How many words can you make from the letters in the word

PAWSTON?

_____ _____

_____ _____

_____ _____

_____ _____

_____ _____

_____ _____

POSSIBLE ANSWERS: Ant, not, pants, past, paws, pots, saw, son, stop, ton, town, was, and wasp.

Connect the dots to see Tag's sweet ride.

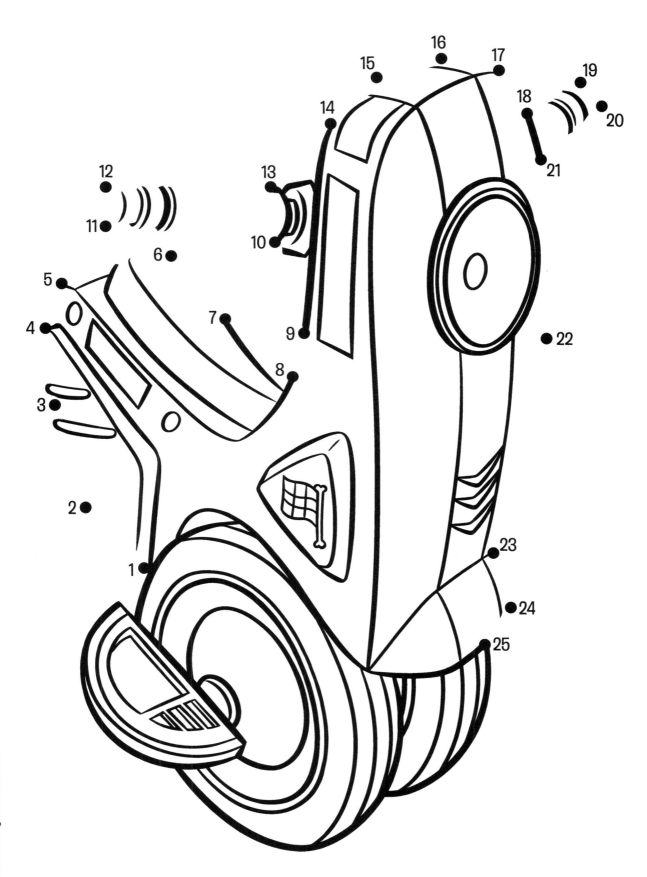

Tag loves to go around town on her scooter.

How do you get around your town? Draw it here.

This is Manhole Dog.
He loves to pop up to say hi!

Tag and Scooch are on their way to the party in the tree.

Follow the letters in the word **PAWSTON** to find your way to their first stop: the ball store.

START
↓

T	R	B	C	P	F	R	M	Y	O
W	O	T	R	A	W	S	T	R	L
V	L	L	Q	T	L	G	O	I	H
U	X	P	O	R	A	D	N	E	D
T	N	O	T	S	W	A	P	F	C
S	P	T	L	K	J	O	T	G	B
Y	A	T	O	N	P	A	W	S	T
X	W	S	W	L	L	V	O	U	O
J	K	M	L	P	O	Q	L	R	N
I	H	G	N	O	T	S	W	A	P

FINISH

Tag and Scooch are stuck in the hedge maze.

Help them get out.

START

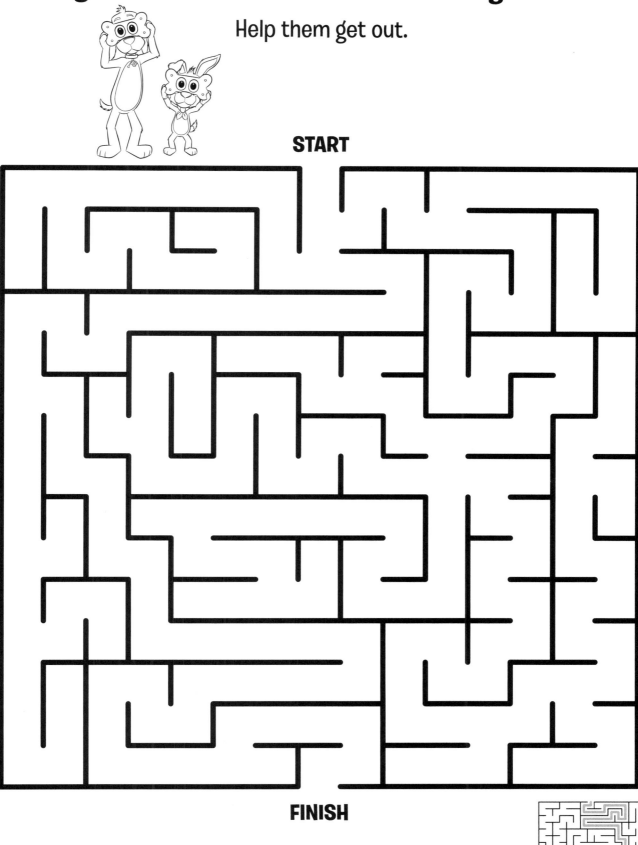

FINISH

ANSWER:

Find the image of the boat that is different from the rest.

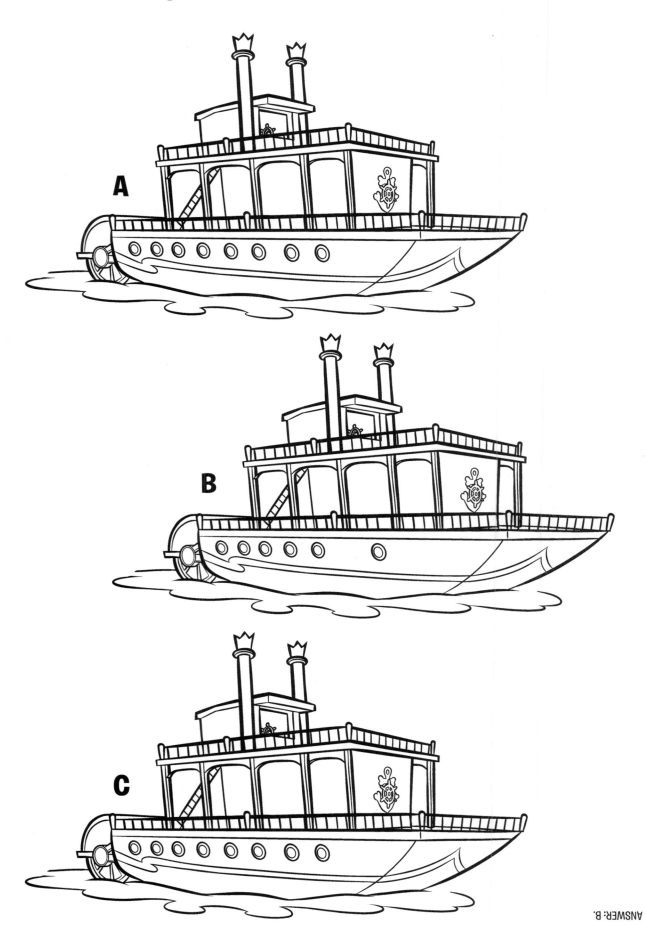

Use A, E, I, O, or U to find these different places in Pawston.

B __ LL ST __ R __

D __ __ RB __ LL ST __ R __

H __ DG __ M __ Z __

B __ G B __ WL D __ N __ R

ANSWERS: Ball store, doorbell store, hedge maze, and Big Bowl Diner.

This is Lady Lydia.
She loves to wear different hats.

Find the image of Lady Lydia that is different from the rest.

ANSWER: E.

What is Lady Lydia saying?

To find out, replace each letter with the one that comes before it in the alphabet. Then write the letters in the blanks.

__ __ __ __ __ __ __ __ __
E P   Z Z P V   M J L F

__ __ __ __ __?
N Z   I B U

This is Tag's mom. She is a pilot.

Connect the dots to see what Tag's mom drives.

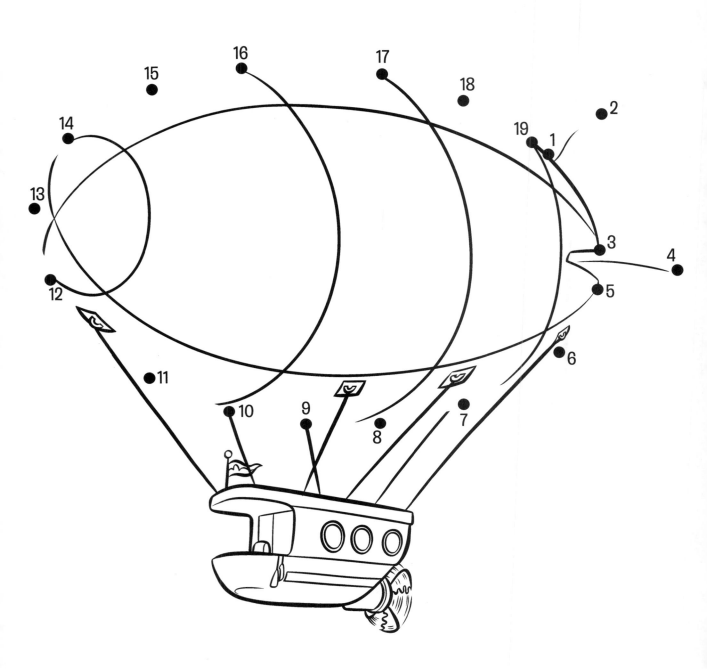

Tag and Scooch are stuck in a blimp traffic jam!

Find the quickest way out.

START

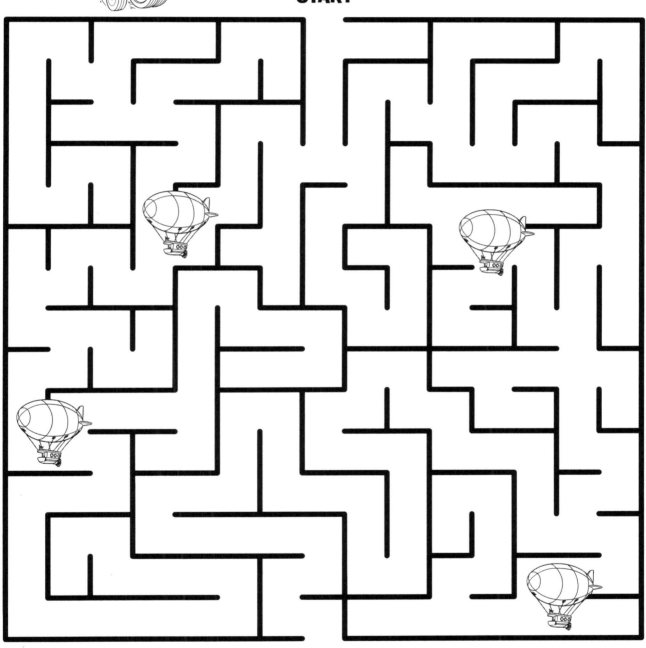

FINISH

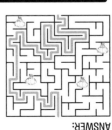

ANSWER:

Scooch uses *bone*-oculars to spot the party in the tree.

Color and decorate your own *bone*-oculars.
Then with the help of an adult,
cut them out to wear on your next adventure!

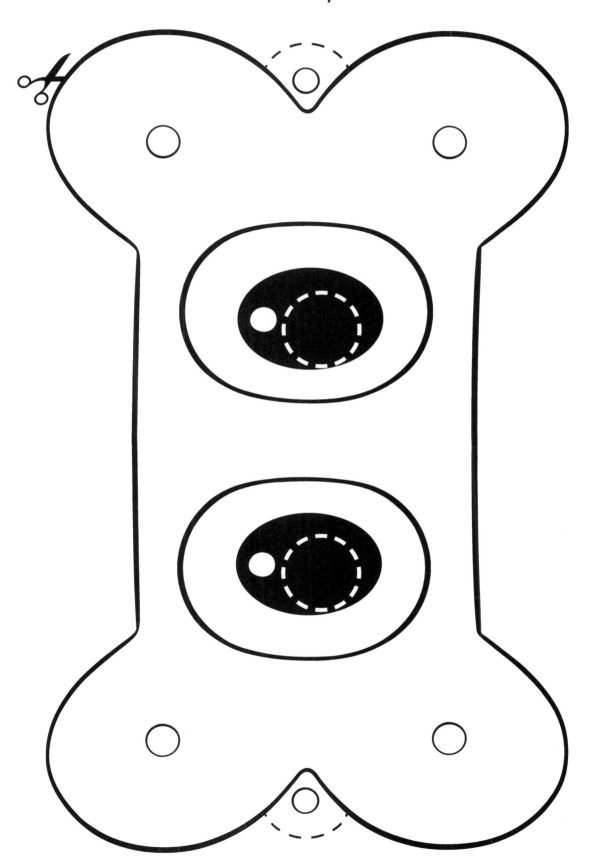

Spot the five differences in the bottom picture.

ANSWERS: The dog on the left is missing, the dog's party hat is missing, a cloud is missing, the juggling dog is missing a ball, and the dog on the right is missing a piece of cake.

Draw yourself at the party in the tree.

Have your own party by decorating these
invitations and giving them to your *paw*-some pals.

To: _____

From: _____

What: _____

When: _____

Where: _____

RSVP: _____

To: _____

From: _____

What: _____

When: _____

Where: _____

RSVP: _____

To: _____

From: _____

What: _____

When: _____

Where: _____

RSVP: _____

To: _____

From: _____

What: _____

When: _____

Where: _____

RSVP: _____

To: _____

From: _____

What: _____

When: _____

Where: _____

RSVP: _____

To: _____

From: _____

What: _____

When: _____

Where: _____

RSVP: _____

To: _____

From: _____

What: _____

When: _____

Where: _____

RSVP: _____

To: _____

From: _____

What: _____

When: _____

Where: _____

RSVP: _____

How many balloons can you count?

ANSWER: 14.

Draw candles and decorations on the cake.

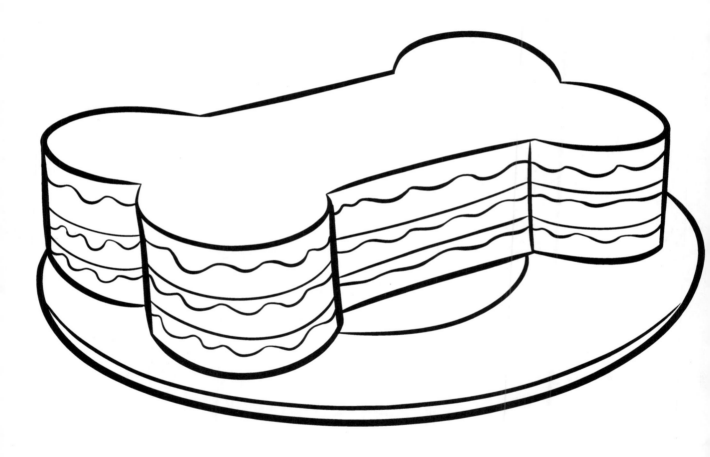

Unscramble the names of Tag and her family.

OMM

_____

IPY

_____

CHREDAD BIUTSIC

_____

GERLIB

_____

PSIKE

_____

AWP

_____

GAT

_____

ANSWERS: Mom, Yip, Cheddar Biscuit, Gilber, Spike, Paw, and Tag.

Cheddar Biscuit is a clown.

Draw yourself as a clown.

Cheddar Biscuit loves to juggle.
Draw some things for her to juggle.

Draw a flower on Lady Lydia's hat.

In Pawston, there are all sorts of dogs.

Draw yourself as a dog.

Spot the five differences in the bottom picture.

Match the dogs to their vehicles.

ANSWER: A-2, B-3, and C-1.

This is Gerald.

To find out his job in Pawston, replace each letter with the one that comes before it in the alphabet. Then write the letters in the blanks.

___ ___ ___ ___ ___ ___ ___ ___
N   B   J   M   E   P   H

Tag and Scooch are helping Gerald deliver the mail.

Can you find the way to the next house?

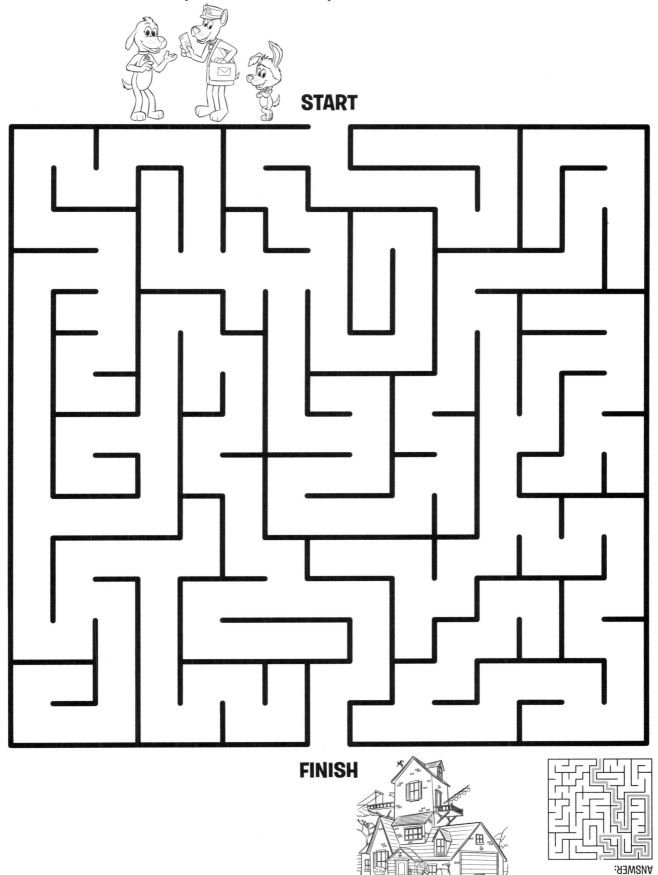

START

FINISH

ANSWER:

The pups love to go to the ball store.

Draw more balls in front of the ball store.

Which bird is different from the rest?

ANSWER: C.

Add rockets to Scooch's tractor to make it go!

This is Tag's father, Paw.
He loves doorbells.

Use the code below to find out the name of Paw's store.

A	B	C	D	E	F	G	H	I	J	K	L	M
1	2	3	4	5	6	7	8	9	10	11	12	13

N	O	P	Q	R	S	T	U	V	W	X	Y	Z
14	15	16	17	18	19	20	21	22	23	24	25	26

___ ___ ___ ___   ___ ___ ___ ___
 4   9   14 7   4   15 14 7

___ ___ ___ ___ ___ ___ ___ ___
 4   15 15 18 2   5   12 12

___ ___ ___ ___ ___
 19 20 15 18 5

Where is Paw going?
Draw it here!

Tag and Scooch have to deliver the mail to Lady Lydia.

Follow the correct path so they don't get chased by the other dogs.

START

FINISH

Draw a new hat for Lady Lydia.

Bone Boxes!

(For two players)

With a friend, take turns drawing a line to connect two paws. If you complete a box, write your initials in it and take another turn. Each player gets one point for a regular box and two points for a bone box. At the end of the game, the player with more points wins!

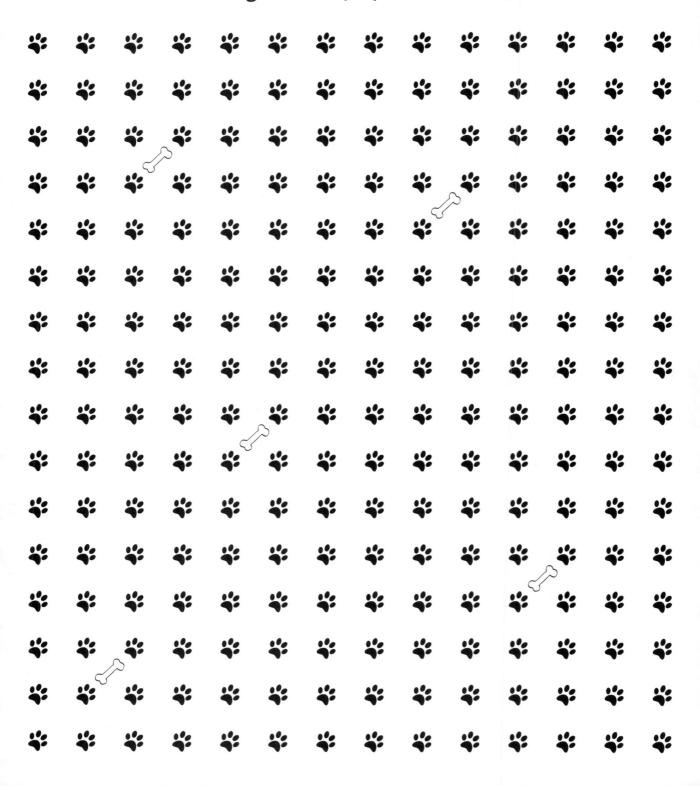

More Bone Boxes!

Match the pups to their dog tags.

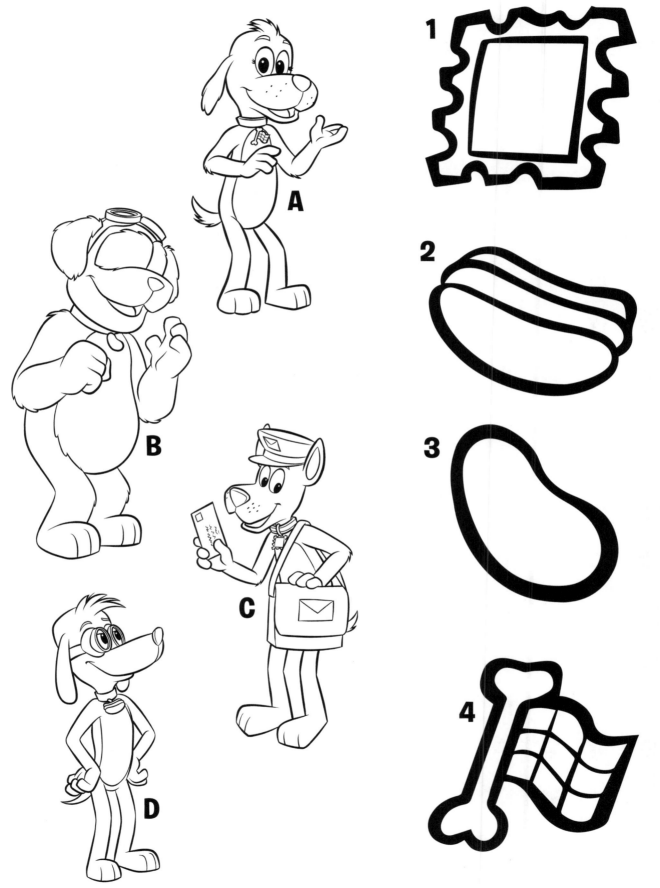

Draw yourself a dog tag here.

Tag loves to create inventions.

If you could invent something, what would it be? Draw it here.

Tag and Scooch like to play ball.

What is your favorite sport?
Draw yourself playing your favorite sport here.

Look up, down, forward, and diagonally to find these words that describe the pups in Pawston.

HELPFUL · CARING · TEAM · KIND · FUN
HOWLING · COMMUNITY · FAMILY · FRIENDLY

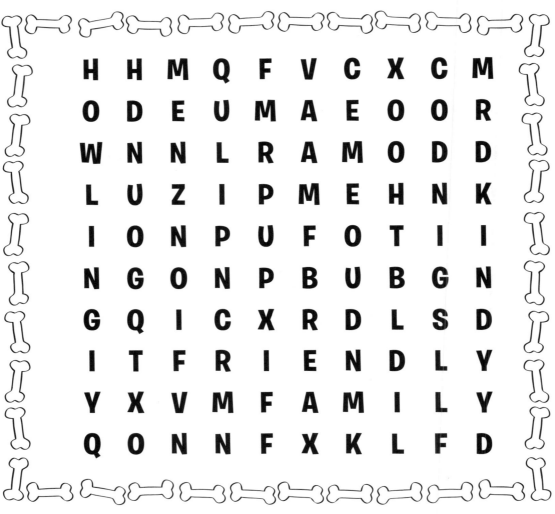

```
H H M Q F V C X C M
O D E U M A E O O R
W N N L R A M O D D
L U Z I P M E H N K
I O N P U F O T I I
N G O N P B U B G N
G Q I C X R D L S D
I T F R I E N D L Y
Y X V M F A M I L Y
Q O N N F X K L F D
```

Connect the dots to see Scooch's stuffed animal, Cluckles the Chicken.

Scooch makes the best *pup*-cakes.

Draw your own *pup*-cake here.

This is Mayor Sniffington.

Draw a bone on her necklace.

Find the names of these pups in the puzzle.
Look up, down, forward, and diagonally.

TAG · SCOOCH · MOM · PAW
FRANK · BEANS · GERALD · SAM

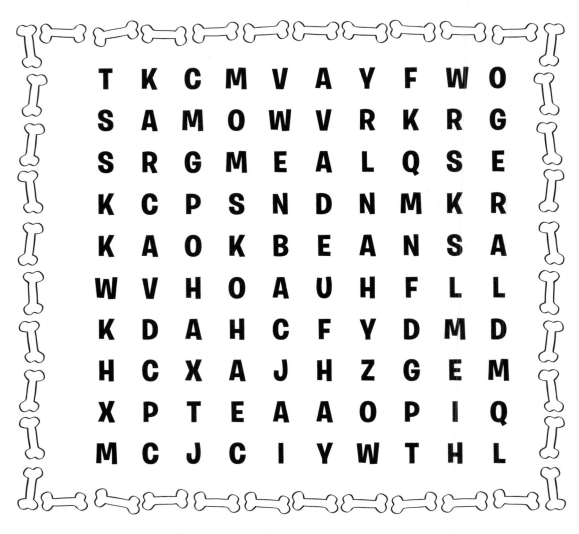

```
T  K  C  M  V  A  Y  F  W  O
S  A  M  O  W  V  R  K  R  G
S  R  G  M  E  A  L  Q  S  E
K  C  P  S  N  D  N  M  K  R
K  A  O  K  B  E  A  N  S  A
W  V  H  O  A  U  H  F  L  L
K  D  A  H  C  F  Y  D  M  D
H  C  X  A  J  H  Z  G  E  M
X  P  T  E  A  A  O  P  I  Q
M  C  J  C  I  Y  W  T  H  L
```

How many times can you find the word **BONES** in the puzzle?

```
N E S E N O B
B O N E S X S
O B O N E S E
N S E N O B N
E B O N E S O
S B S E N O B
B O N E S E S
N O S E N O B
```

ANSWER: 10.

Match each pup to their shadow.

Draw your favorite pup!

This is Grandmaw and Grandpaw.
They are Tag's grandparents.

Where do Grandmaw and Grandpaw work?

Use the code to find out.

A	B	C	D	E	F	G	H	I	J	K	L	M
1	2	3	4	5	6	7	8	9	10	11	12	13

N	O	P	Q	R	S	T	U	V	W	X	Y	Z
14	15	16	17	18	19	20	21	22	23	24	25	26

___ ___ ___ ___ ___ ___ ___
16   1   23 19 20 15 14

___ ___ ___ ___ ___ ___ ___ ___ ___ ___ ___
16 1 23 20 15 13 15 20 9 22 5

___ ___ ___ ___ ___ ___
7   1   18 1   7   5

ANSWER: Pawston Pawtomotive Garage.

Where are Tag and Scooch going?

Draw it!

Pawston is a place where everyone is helpful.

Write about a time when you were helpful.

_____

_____

_____

_____

_____

_____

_____

The Barkapellas are dogs who love to sing.

What is your favorite type of music?

_____

What is your favorite song?

_____

Who is your favorite musical artist?

_____

Draw yourself singing!

Write your own song here.

_____

_____

_____

_____

_____

_____

_____

_____

_____

_____

_____

_____

_____

Bacon is Beans's favorite treat.

Draw your favorite things to eat.

Who's who in Pawston?

Use the clues to find the names of these Pawston pups.

1. Maildog

_____

2. Blimp pilot

_____

3. Race car driver

_____

4. Doorbell store owner

_____

How many times can you find the word **PAWSTON** in the puzzle below?

```
P A N O T S W A P
A P A W S T O N A
W N O T S W A P W
S P A W S T O N S
T N O T S W A P T
O P A W S T O N O
N N O T S W A P N
P A W S T O N A W
N O T S W A P W A
A P A W S T O N P
```

Tag and her friends love to howl when they're happy.

What makes you happy?

Draw it here!

Welcome to Pawston!

Tag and Scooch are best friends.

Who is your best friend?

_____

What is your favorite thing to do with your best friend?

_____

Describe why you like your best friend.

_____

_____

Draw you and your best friend here.

Help Frank get to Beans.

START

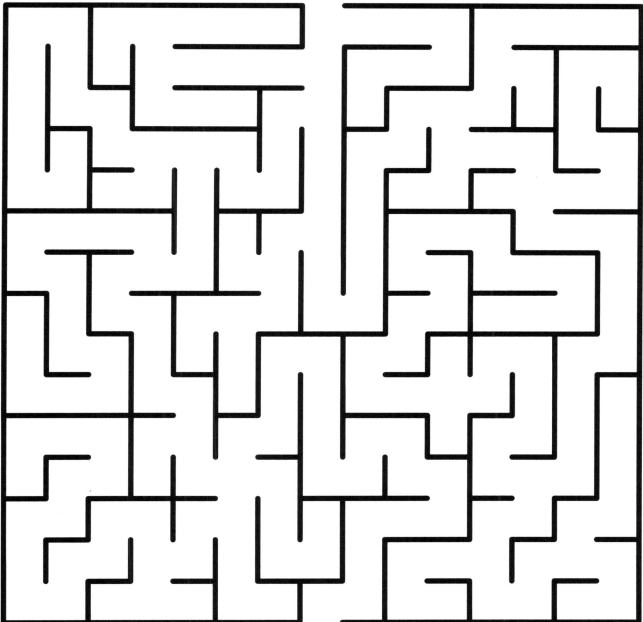

FINISH

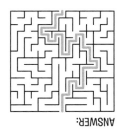

ANSWER:

Draw Lady Lydia a new hat.

Learn to draw Tag

Help Tag get back home.

START

FINISH

What are Tag and Scooch saying?

Tag needs to find Scooch.

Which path will lead Tag to Scooch?

A

B

C

What is Frank saying to Beans?

The pups love to live in Pawston.

Draw where you live.

Where is Tag going? Draw it!

Who is this?

To find out, replace each letter with the one
that comes before it in the alphabet.

T B N

X I J Q Q F U

Circle the picture of Tag that matches the one on the left.

A

B

C

ANSWER: C.

Where is Scooch going?

Draw it here!

How many times can you find the word **PUPS** in the puzzle below?

```
P P U S P U P
U U P U P S U
P P U S P U P
S S P U P S S
S P U S P U P
P P U P S P U
U P U S P U P
P U P S U P S
```

ANSWER: 13.

Fill in the missing letters to spell the names of these pups:

T _ g

Y _ p

C _ _ e d _ _ a r   Bi _ _ cui _ _

Gi _ _ be _ _

S _ _ i _ _ e

S _ _ _ _ o _ _ h

Pawston Memory Game

Look carefully at this picture,
then turn the page.

How much do you remember about the picture on the previous page?

1. How many dogs are on the page?

_____

2. What is Yip riding?

_____

3. What is on Yip's pacifier?

_____

4. How many trees are there?

_____

5. Is Scooch in the picture?

_____

Draw a chicken on Scooch's tractor.

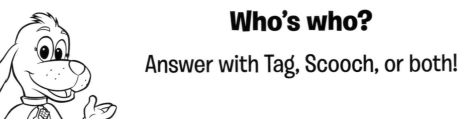

Who's who?

Answer with Tag, Scooch, or both!

1. Who likes to invent things?

_____

2. Who makes *paw*-some *pup*-cakes?

_____

3. Who likes to go?

_____

4. Who drives a tractor?

_____

5. Who used to live on a farm?

_____

6. Who is very helpful?

_____

ANSWERS: 1. Tag, 2. Scooch, 3. Both, 4. Scooch, 5. Scooch, and 6. Both.

Connect the dots to see Tag and Scooch's big surprise.

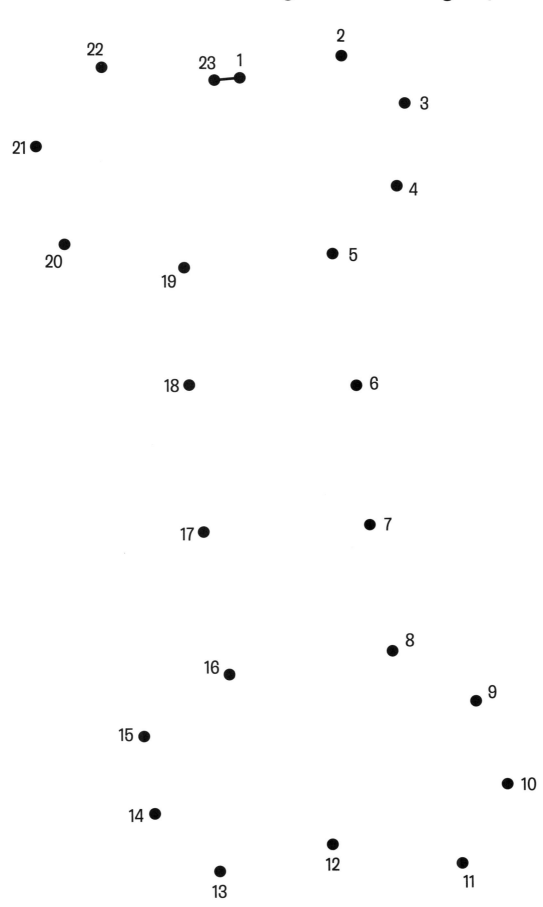

Draw mustaches on Tag and Scooch so they look like Sam Whippet.

Draw a picture of yourself with a mustache.

Sam Whippet has lost the key to his car.

Use the code to find out where Tag and Scooch look for the key.

A	B	C	D	E	F	G	H	I	J	K	L	M
1	2	3	4	5	6	7	8	9	10	11	12	13

N	O	P	Q	R	S	T	U	V	W	X	Y	Z
14	15	16	17	18	19	20	21	22	23	24	25	26

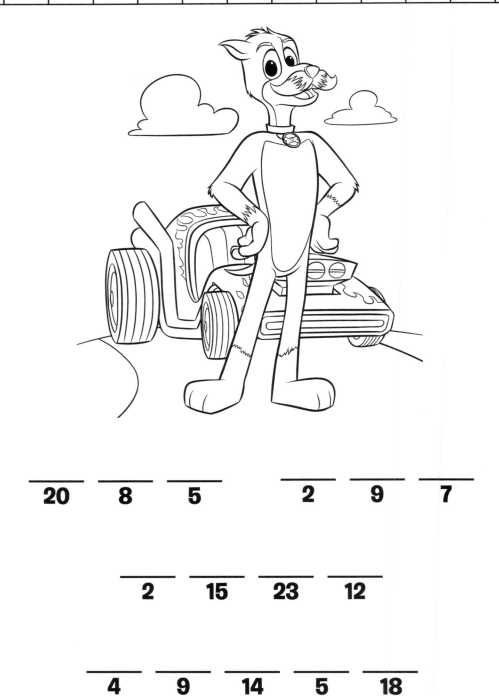

___ ___ ___   ___ ___ ___
20 8   5   2   9   7

___ ___ ___ ___
2   15 23 12

___ ___ ___ ___ ___
4   9   14 5   18

Tag and Scooch find all sorts of things at the Big Bowl Diner.

Match each item to its shadow.

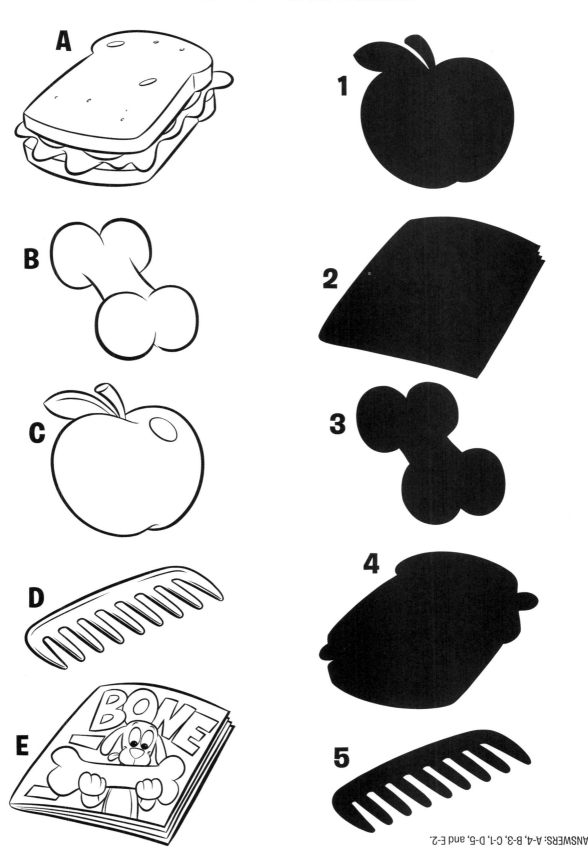

A

B

C

D

E

1

2

3

4

5

Where are Frank and Beans going? Draw it!

What do these pups need to do to find Sam's key?

To find out, replace each letter with the one that comes before it in the alphabet. Then write the letters in the blanks.

X P S L

U P H F U I F S

ANSWER: Work together.

Follow the correct path for Tag and his friends to find Sam's key.

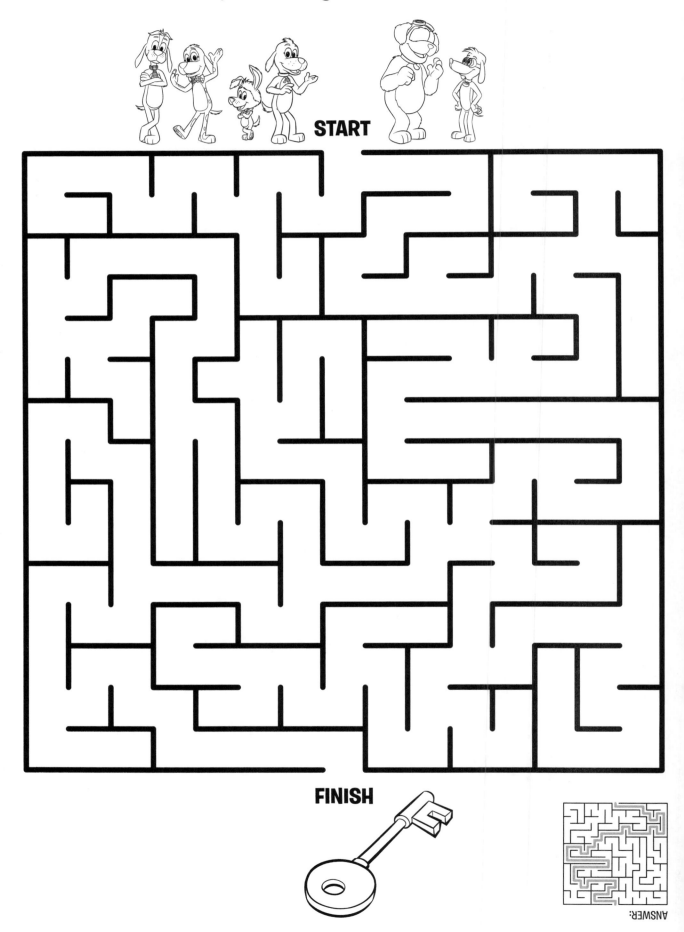

START

FINISH

Now there are too many keys.

Find the key that is different from the rest.
That's the one that starts Sam's car!

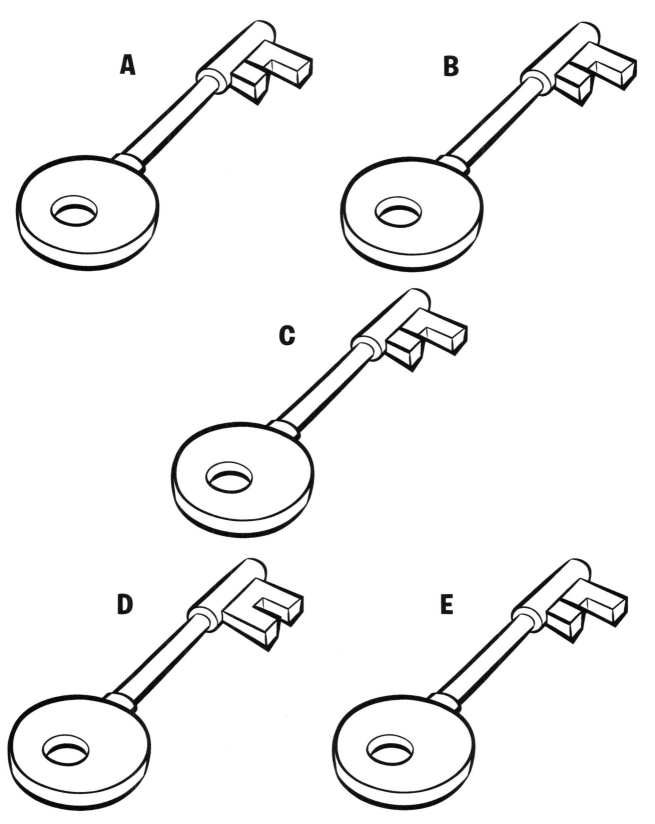

ANSWER: D.

Where is Sam going? Draw it!

Tag builds a brand-new car.

Starting at the arrow, go clockwise and write every other letter in the blanks to find out the name of Tag's car.

Connect the dots to see the Barker Buggy.

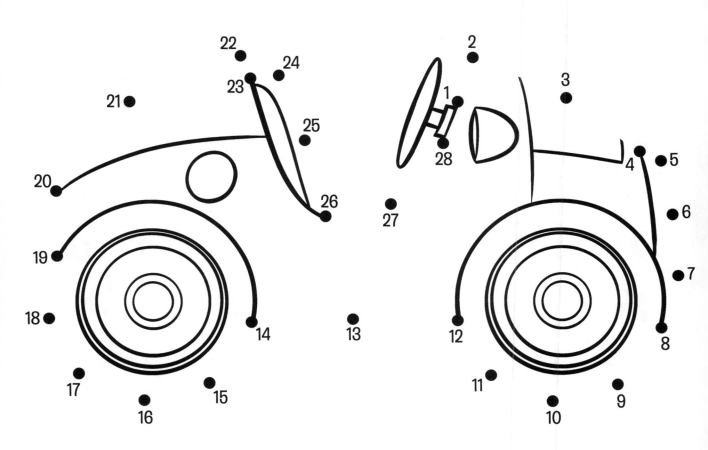

Draw your favorite car here.

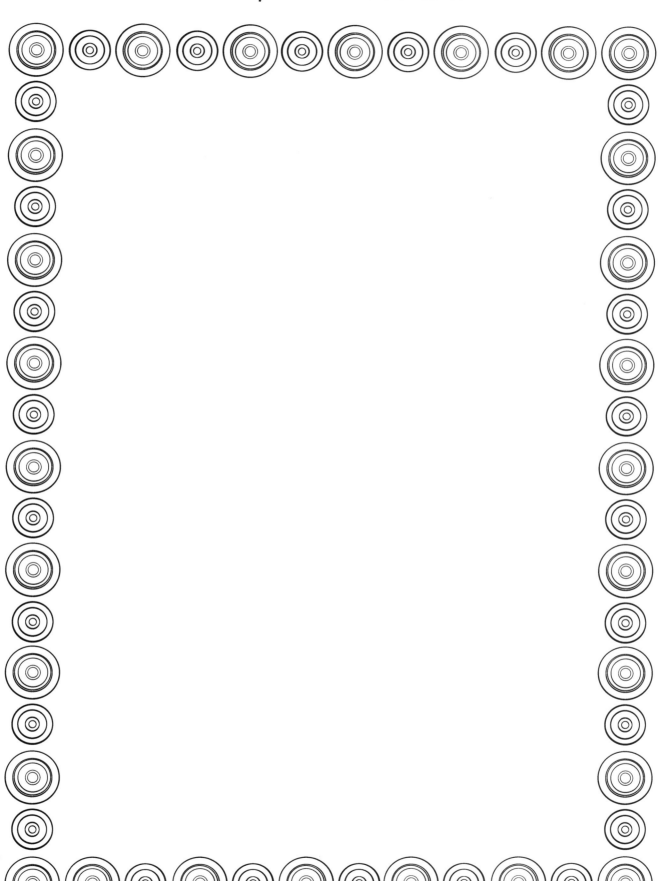

Tag's new car has lots of gadgets and gizmos.

What kind of gadgets would your car have? Draw them here.

Tag loves treats.

How many Bow-Wow Bones can you count?

Use the number key below to color Cheddar Biscuit.

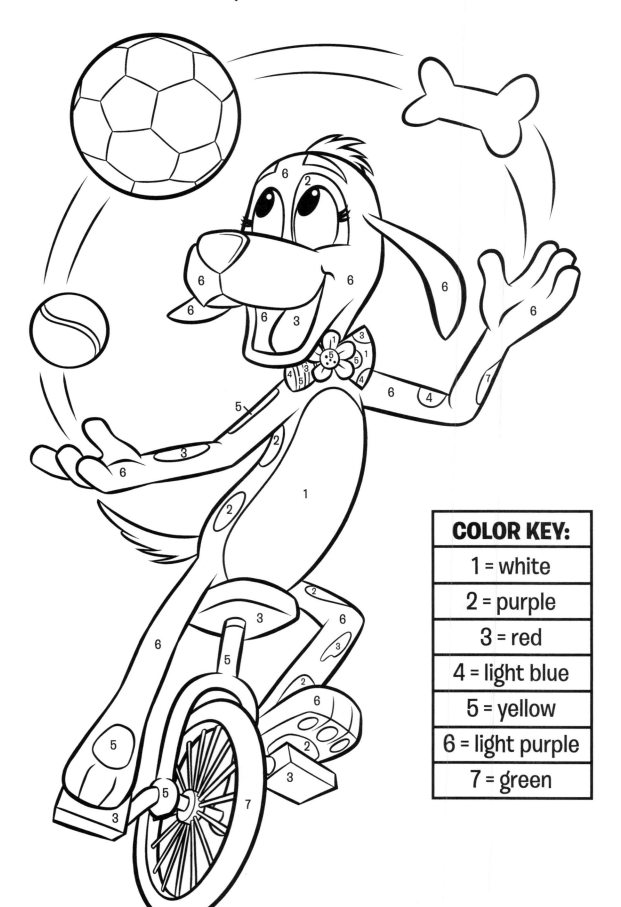

COLOR KEY:

1 = white
2 = purple
3 = red
4 = light blue
5 = yellow
6 = light purple
7 = green

How many circus pups can you draw to fit in Tag's Barker Buggy?

Draw balloons on Tag's car to make it fly.

Tag and Scooch run across Bone Bridge!

These three teams are in a race.

Follow the lines to see which team wins.

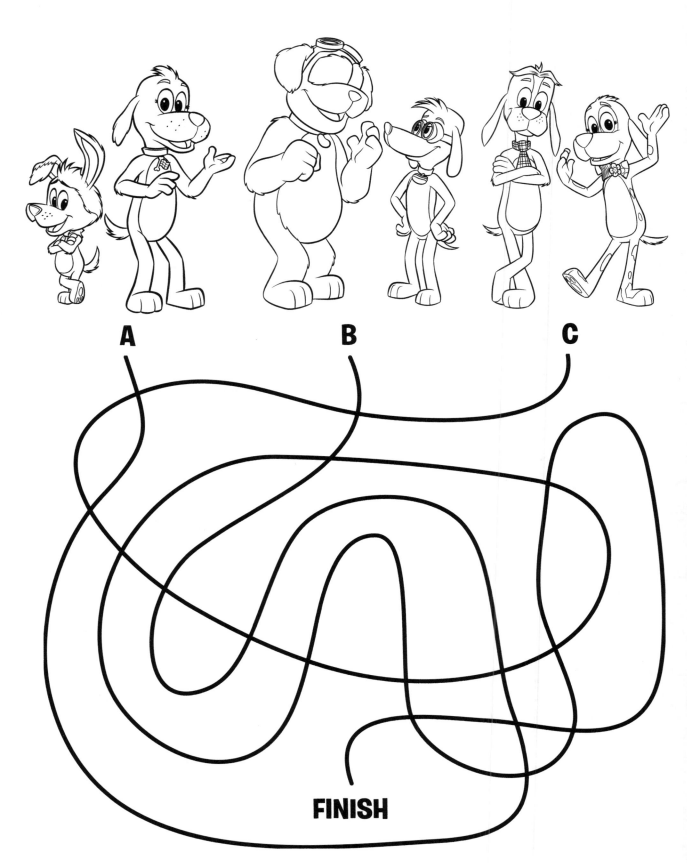

A

B

C

FINISH

Use the code to find out what Tag and Scooch need to finish the race.

A	W	T	R	K	E	M	O

ANSWER: Teamwork.

Tag

Scooch

Frank and Beans

Lady Lydia

Cheddar Biscuit

Gilber

Mom and Paw

Grandmaw and Grandpaw

Sam Whippet

Gerald

Match these pups to their names.

A. Tag

B. Scooch

C. Cheddar Biscuit

D. Gilber

E. Frank

F. Beans

G. Gerald

H. Lady Lydia

I. Manhole Dog

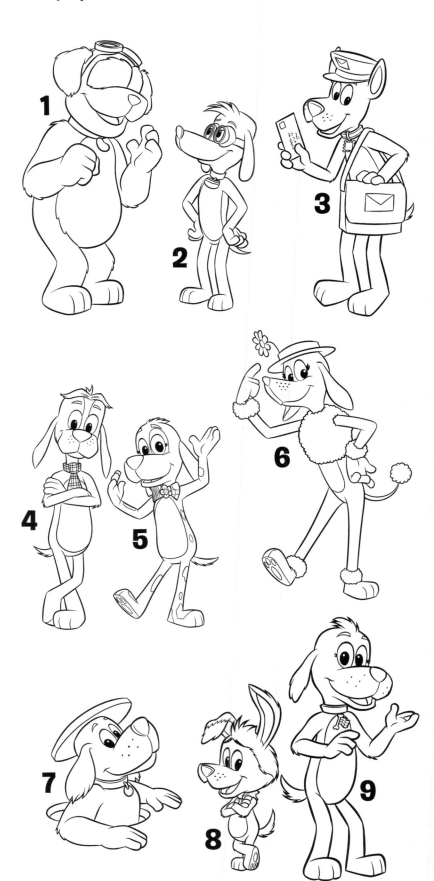

Paw-some Pals

Go, Dog. Go!